THE GREEDY LITTLE COBBLER

by Tony Ross

Andersen Press · London

Long ago, a little cobbler lived in a little town.
Everybody in the town loved the cobbler and day after day,
he would sit at his last mending their shoes.
Nobody had much money, so sometimes the cobbler would
take a pig in payment for a pair of shoes, or an egg for
a new heel.
Of course, the little cobbler wasn't rich, but he had lots of
eggs and bacon for his supper.

Sometimes the little cobbler would make a new pair of shoes for the farmer, and in return would get a load of leather.
Or he might put new soles on the blacksmith's boots, and the blacksmith would give him nails, or sharpen his tools.
That's what life was like in the little town, with everybody helping everybody else.
In the evenings the cobbler would sit with his good friends and think, "Life's not bad!"

One day, the little cobbler was passing a rich man's house, when he happened to peep over the hedge. The rich man's friends were playing about in the garden.

"Hmm," muttered the cobbler, "my life may be good, but it certainly looks better to be rich!" There and then, the greedy little man decided to mend only the finest shoes. He would ask for LOTS of money in return, and accept no more pigs and eggs.

As the fine lords would not come to the cobbler, he had to go to them. He built himself a little cart and loaded his cobbler's things onto it.

A poor shepherd came to him, asking for a new boot in exchange for a lamb.

"On your way," laughed the cobbler. "I've better boots to mend now!"

At the first great house the cobbler visited, the servants set the dogs on him.

"Not a good start!" gasped the cobbler, scrambling to safety on his cart.

Next, the little cobbler visited the richest lord in the land. He found him in the garden, playing with his falcon.
It happened that the lord's shoes were wearing thin, so the cobbler put on new soles and heels. The work done, he asked for a silver shilling.
"Away with you, sir!" snapped the lord. "I *never* pay tradesmen, it's an honor to work for me. Why, when it becomes known you mend *my* shoes, you'll get all the work you want!"

"Jolly nice of the lord to let me mend his shoes free!"
muttered the cobbler as he trudged off towards the
colonel's house.
The colonel wanted a new pair of red boots, to wear with his
new blue uniform.
The cobbler made the boots from the finest leather.
Putting them on, the colonel leaped on his horse.
"The war's just started!" he yelled, galloping off into
the night.
Of course, the colonel had forgotten to pay the cobbler.

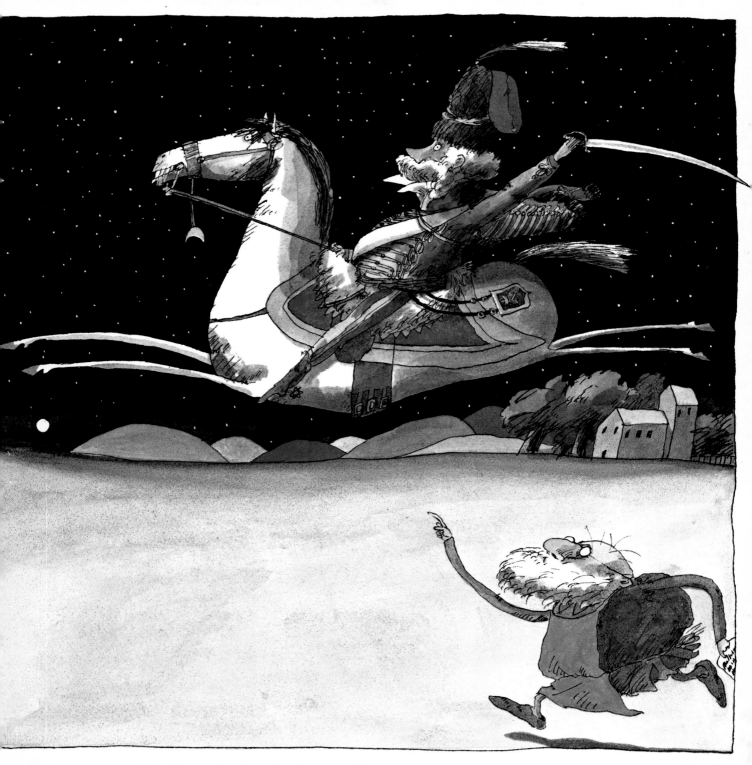

As the admiral was in port, the cobbler paid him a visit.
"NEW SEABOOTS, THAT'S THE THING!" boomed
the admiral.
The seaboots took a week to make, and they were the most
handsome, and the most waterproof boots on the sea.
The admiral was delighted. So delighted, in fact, he sailed
away without even remembering to pay the little cobbler.

"Never mind," thought the cobbler, "I now have lots of rich customers. One day I *must* be rich too!"
He made a pair of ballet shoes for the most famous ballerina in the world. They were silver, with pink ribbons and hard toes.
The ballerina was overjoyed.
"They're so comfy," she trilled. "I must dance right away!"
And she did! She danced in the theater that evening, watched by the little cobbler. He hoped she would remember to pay for the shoes after the performance. But when the curtain came down, he never saw her again.

That evening the little cobbler sat all alone in his little shop. Not one of his fine customers had given him a penny, and by this time he had no leather or nails left.

He had no food, or money to buy any, so he was trying to fry an old boot for his supper.

"Oh dear," he wailed, "getting rich has only made me poor." He just sat there and sobbed.

One by one, his old friends gathered by the window to see what all the noise was about.

"And my feet hurt!" howled the greedy little cobbler.

"No wonder!" cried his old friends, pointing to the floor. "Look at your shoes!"

The cobbler looked. His shoes were in tatters, quite worn away with pushing his cart from house to house.

It was too much; the cobbler collapsed again in tears.

"I'd still like you to make me a new boot in exchange for the lamb," said the shepherd shyly. "That is, if you've nothing better to do."

The cobbler dried his eyes, and beamed.

"There's nothing better than working for old friends," he said.

In no time at all, the little cobbler had a HUGE pile of shoes to mend.

Of course, he was still paid with pigs and eggs, or sometimes a goose or a hen. But now it didn't seem to matter, as he felt richer than he'd ever felt before. He had plenty to eat again, lots of leather and nails, and more important, he had all his old friends.

Amid all this happy work, the little cobbler could never find the time to make a new pair of shoes for himself.

"D'ye know," he'd often say to strangers, with a merry grin, "THE COBBLER'S ALWAYS THE WORST SHOD!"